The Dog Child

by Simon Black

Illustrated by Honorio Robledo

Cinco Puntos Press
www.cincopuntos.com

Mr. and Mrs. McVitie loved their dog soooo much. Her name was Judy, and she slept in the bed between them.

"How's our baby doing?" Mr. McVitie would say when he came home from work. Mrs. McVitie would answer, "I think our baby is a little hungry. Let's give her a cookie." The McVities would feed their dog cookies and ice cream and all kinds of things that dogs aren't supposed to eat, but Judy seemed to like eating them just fine.

"Look what a nice pair of pajamas I've made for our baby," Mrs. McVitie said one day.
"Isn't she beautiful in them?" Mr. McVitie said.

And they took a video of their Judy parading around in her pajamas.
After that, Judy always wore clothes.

"You know what?" Mr. McVitie said one day. "I think it's time our baby girl went to school."

"You are so right," said Mrs. McVitie. "We'll take her to school tomorrow."

So they did. But they didn't take her to a dog school—no!—because they thought Judy was a child just like other children.

"We're here to place our daughter in kindergarten," said Mr. McVitie.

The teacher looked at Judy, all dressed up in her little plaid school skirt and holding a little lunch pail in her mouth. She understood then that the McVities were…well…a little…unusual.

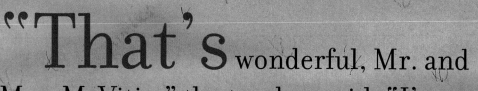

"That's wonderful, Mr. and Mrs. McVitie," the teacher said. "I'm sure Judy will be very happy here."

The McVities waved goodbye. They were a little sad. And Judy was a little nervous. She'd never been left on her own before.

But the teacher made everything all right. She led Judy up to the front of the classroom and announced, "Class, we're going to have our own dog!"

"I see you're starting T-ball next week," Mr. McVitie said to the teacher one day after class. "I think it would be good for Judy to get involved in sports."

So Judy joined the T-ball team. She couldn't hold the bat very well, but she was tremendous in the field.

Then it was time for Judy's sixth birthday party. So the McVities called the parents of all the other children in Judy's class and said, "It's our daughter's birthday, and we'd be honored if you and your child would come to her party."

The other parents laughed about it behind the McVities' backs. Mrs. McVitie was shopping for the party when she heard some of the ladies talking about it in the other aisle.

"Do they really think that dog is a child? They're so nutty. Ha ha ha!"

Mrs. McVitie felt sorry for them because she
saw that they didn't understand. But she made lovely tarts
for the b-day party just the same. And all the children
sang *Happy Birthday* as Mr. McVitie brought out the
birthday cake.

Mr. McVitie noticed the kids' parents weren't singing
along. "Why aren't you singing?" he asked.

"Well," coughed the bravest father, who happened
to be the mayor. "I don't mind singing, but not to a dog."

"To a what?" Mr. McVitie exclaimed. He was shocked.

"Well, that's what she is, McVitie," said the mayor.
"She's a canine."

Mr. McVitie scrunched up his fists. His wife could tell he was about to hit somebody, so she hurried over.

"Go ahead, Judy," she said loudly. "Blow out the candles and make a wish."

Judy just sat there.

"Come on, Judy," coaxed Mrs. McVitie. "We're all waiting to eat the cake. Blow out the candles, sweetheart."

But Judy just sat there in her birthday outfit doing nothing. The parents started whispering to each other. "That dog is never going to blow out the candles," one father declared. "Dogs can't blow. They don't have the lips for it. And they can't make wishes either."

"All right, kids," all the other parents said. "It's time to go home."

The children didn't want to go though. They really loved Judy. They jumped up and down and tried to help her.

"Come on, Judy! Blow out the candles, would you!"
They tried to show her how to blow. "Just put your
lips together, Judy! Like this!"

But Judy didn't seem to understand. She just sat there looking confused.

"Come on, kids," the parents said for the last time. And everybody was about to leave, when Judy jumped up on the table.

"Yahoo!" yelled the kids. "She's going to blow out the candles!"

Suddenly Judy turned around and put her back to the cake.

"Oh boy, what's that mutt gonna do now?" said one of the fathers. He thought Judy was going to poop on the cake.

And then Judy started wagging her tail. She wagged and wagged until it was like a helicopter blade above the cake. It made a mighty wind that woooooooshed over the candles, and when the parents looked, every candle was out!

"Hooray for Judy!" the children hollered. The McVities were very proud. Even the mayor was amused. He went up to Mr. McVitie and slapped him on the back.

"That's one heck of a dog—I mean, daughter—you've got there, McVitie."

"Hey, Judy, what'd you wish for?" someone yelled.

"She can't tell you that," one of the kids said. "If she tells her wish, it won't come true."

But, if you had looked at Judy's eyes right then, you would have seen that they were gleaming with a magical glow because she was wishing very hard that her secret wish would come true.

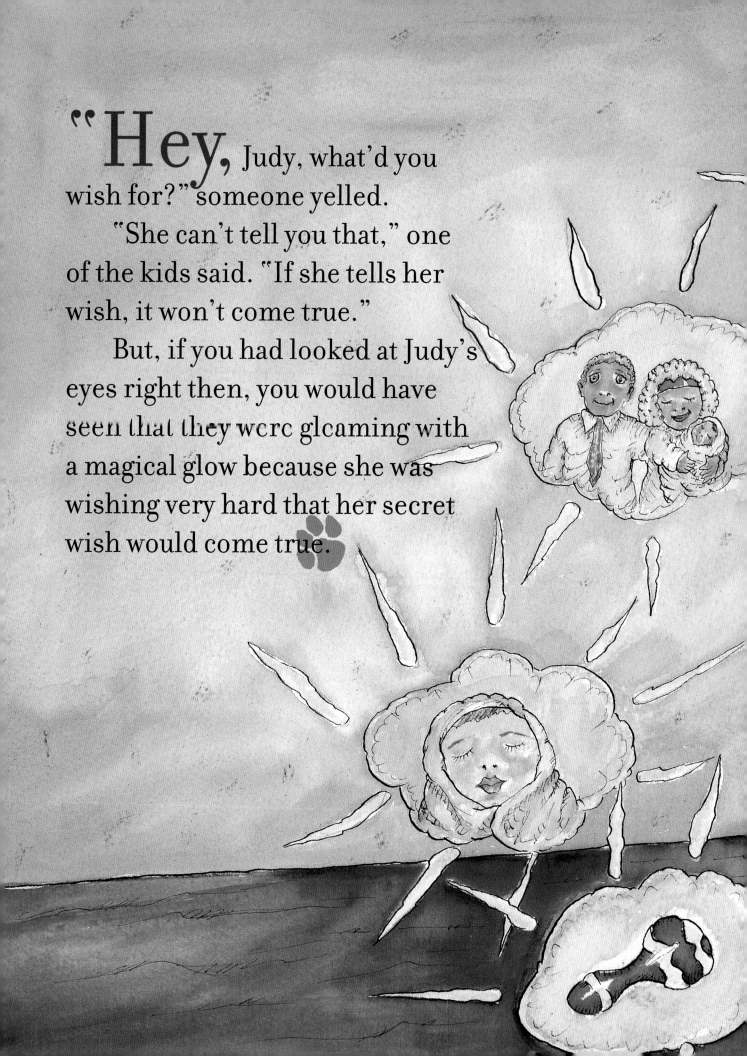

And nine months later it did! The McVities finally had a real baby, and Judy didn't have to wear those crazy clothes around anymore. She could go back to being a dog.

But she still slept in their bed between them and ate cookies and did a bunch of stuff dogs aren't supposed to do.

And they all lived happily ever after.

The Real Judy!

Printed in Hong Kong.

First Edition
10 9 8 7 6 5 4 3 2 1

Library of Congress Cataloging-in-Publication Data

Black, Simon.
Dog child / by Simon Black ; with illustrations by Honorio Robledo.
p. cm.
Summary: The McVities love their dog Judy so much that they dress her up, send her to school, and throw her a birthday party as if she were human.
ISBN-13 978-0-938317-42-5 ; ISBN-10 0-938317-42-3 (hardback : alk. paper) [1. Dogs—Fiction. 2. Humorous stories.] I. Robledo, Honorio, ill. II. Title.
PZ7.B5296Dog 2006
[E]--dc22
2005023613

To my children Vivien and Archie and to my nephews Dillon, Griffin, Callum and Robert— Simon Black

To my children Nico, Amalia, and Tajira— Honorio Robledo

Book and cover design by Antonio Castro H.

Thanks to Honorio for bringing Dog Child to Cinco Puntos.